Thomas Morton

Three Weeks after Marriage

Thomas Morton

Three Weeks after Marriage

ISBN/EAN: 9783337336936

Printed in Europe, USA, Canada, Australia, Japan

Cover: Foto ©Andreas Hilbeck / pixelio.de

More available books at **www.hansebooks.com**

Three Weeks after Marriage;

A

C O M E · D Y,

In T W O A C T S,

AS PERFORMED AT THE

T H E A T R E - R O Y A L

In C O V E N T - G A R D E N.

——— Otium & oppidi
Laudat rura fui———
HOR.
——— Nugæ feria ducent
In mala———
HOR.

L O N D O N:

Printed and Sold by E. JOHNSON, between No. 4 and 5,
Ludgate Hill.

[PRICE ONE SHILLING.]

ADVERTISEMENT.

THE following Farce was offered to the public in January 1764; but the quarrel about a trifle, and the renewal of that quarrel after the difpute had fubfided, being thought unnatural, the piece was *damned*. Mr. LEWIS of Covent-Garden Theatre, had the good tafte to revive it for his benefit, with an alteration of the title, and it has been fince repeated with fuccefs. A fimilar incident happened to VOLTAIRE at PARIS. That writer, in the year 1734, produced a tragedy, intitled ADELAIDE DU GUESCLIN, which was hiffed through every act. In 1765, LE KAIN, an actor of eminence, revived the play, which had lain for years under condemnation. Every fcene was applauded. What can I think, fays VOLTAIRE, of thefe oppofite judgements? He tells the following anecdote. A banker at Paris had orders to get a new march compofed for one of the regiments of Charles XII. He employed a man of talents for the purpofe. The march was prepared and a practice of it had at the banker's houfe before a numerous affembly. The mufic was found deteftable. MOURET (that was the compofer's name) retired with his performance, and foon after inferted it in one of his operas. The banker and his friends went to the opera; the march was applauded. *Ah; fays the banker, that's what we wanted: why did you not give us fomething in this tafte?* Sir, replied MOURET, the march which you now applaud, is the very fame that you condemned before.

Dra-

Dramatis Personæ.

M E N.

Sir CHARLES RACKETT,	Mr. LEWIS.
DRUGGET,	Mr. QUICK.
LOVELACE,	Mr. PALMER.
WOODLEY,	Mr. CUBITT.

W O M E N.

Lady RACKETT,	Mrs. ABINGTON.
Mrs. DRUGGET,	Mrs. PITT.
NANCY,	Mrs. MORTON.
DIMITY,	Mrs. WILSON.

A SERVANT, &c.

Three

Three Weeks after Marriage.

Table. 2 Chairs SC T I.

Enter Woodley *and* Dimity. *L. H*

Dimity.

PO! Po!------no fuch thing------I tell you, Mr. Woodley, you are a mere novice in thefe affairs.

Wood. Nay, but liften to reafon, Mrs. Dimity,--- has not your mafter, Mr. Drugget, invited me down to his country-feat, in order to give me his daughter Nancy in marriage; and with what pretence can he now break off?

Dim. What pretence!-----you put a body out of all patience----But go on your own way, Sir; my advice is all loft upon you.

Wood. You do me injuftice, Mrs. Dimity---- your advice has governed my whole conduct---Have not I fixed an intereft in the young lady's heart?

Dim. An intereft in a fiddleftick!-----you ought to have made love to the father and mother---what, do you think the way to get a wife, at this time of day, is by fpeaking fine things to the lady you have a fancy for?---That was the practice, indeed; but things are alter'd now---you muft addrefs the old people, Sir; and never trouble your head about

B   your

your miftrefs---None of your letters, and verfes, and loft looks, and fine fpeeches,----" Have compaffion, though angelic creature, on a poor dying," ---Pfhaw! ftuff! nonfenfe! all out of fafhion,---- Go your ways to the old curmudgeon, humour his whims---" I fhall efteem it an honour, Sir, to be allied to a gentleman of your rank and tafte." " Upon my word, he's a pretty young gentleman." -----Then wheel about to the mother: " Your daughter, Ma'am, is the very model of you, and I fhall adore her for your fake." " Here, come hither, Nancy, take this gentleman for better for worfe." " La, mama, I can never confent."---- " I fhould not have thought of your confent---the confent of your relations is enough : why, how now, huffey!" So away you go to church, the knot is tied, an agreeable honey-moon follows, the charm is then diffolv'd ; you go to all the clubs in St. James's Street ; your lady goes to the Coterie ; and, in a little time you both go to Doctor's Commons ; and, if faults on both fides prevent a divorce, you'll quarrel like contrary elements all the reft of your lives.---- that's the way of the world now.

Wood. But you know, my dear Dimity, the old couple have received every mark of attention from me.

Dim. Attention! to be fure you did not fall afleep in their company ; but what then ?----You fhould have entered into their characters, play'd with their humours, and facrificed to their abfurdities.

Wood. But if my temper is too frank---

Dim. Frank, indeed! yes, you have been frank enough to ruin yourfelf.---Have not you to do with a rich old fhop-keeper, retired from bufinefs with an hundred thoufand pounds in his pocket, to enjoy the duft of the London road, which he calls living

in

in the country----and yet you muſt find fault with
his ſituation!----What if he has made a ridiculous
gimcrack of his houſe and gardens, you know his
heart is ſet upon it; and could not you have com-
mended his taſte? But you muſt be too frank!----
"Thoſe walks and alleys are too regular----thoſe
evergreens ſhould not be cut into ſuch fantaſtic
ſhapes."---And thus you adviſe a poor old me-
chanic, who delights in every thing that's monſtrous,
to follow nature----Oh, you're likely to be a ſuc-
ceſsful lover!

Wood. But why ſhould I not ſave a father-in-law
from being a laughing-ſtock?

Dim. Make him your father-in-law firſt---

Wood. Why, he can't open his windows for the
duſt---he ſtands all day looking through a pane of
glaſs at the carts and ſtage-coaches as they paſs by,
and he calls that living in the freſh air, and enjoying his own thoughts.

Dim. And could not you let him go on his own
way? You have ruin'd yourſelf by talking ſenſe to
him, and all your nonſenſe to the daughter won't
make amends for it---And then the mother; how
have you play'd your cards in that quarter?---She
wants a tinſel man of faſhion for her ſecond daugh-
ter----"Don't you ſee (ſays ſhe) how happy my
eldeſt girl is made by marrying Sir Charles Rackett.
She has been married three entire weeks, and not ſo
much as one angry word has paſs'd between them --
Nancy ſhall have a man of quality too."

Wood. And yet I know Sir Charles Rackett perfectly well.

Dim. Yes, ſo do I; and I know he'll make his
lady wretched at laſt---But what then? You ſhould
have humour'd the old folks,----you ſhould have
been a talking empty fop, to the good old lady,

and

and to the old gentleman, an admirer of his tafte in gardening. But you have loft him---he is grown fond of this beau Lovelace, who is here in the houfe with him; the coxcomb ingratiates himfelf by flattery, and you're undone by franknefs.

Wood. And yet, Dimity, I won't defpair.

Dim. And yet you have reafon to defpair; a million of reafons----To-morrow is fix'd for the wedding-day; Sir Charles and his lady are to be here this very night---they are engag'd, indeed, at a great rout in town, but they take a bed here, notwithstanding.----The family is fitting up for them; Mr. Drugget will keep you all up in the next room there, till they arrive---and to-morrow the bufinefs is over----and yet you don't. defpair !----hufh !----hold your tongue; here comes Lovelace.---Step in, and I'll devife fomething, I warrant you. (*Exit M.* Woodley) The old folks fhall not have their own way---'tis enough to vex a body, to fee an old father and mother marrying their daughter as they pleafe, in fpite of all I can do.   [*Exit.*

Enter Drugget and Lovelace.

Drug. And fo you like my houfe and gardens, Mr. Lovelace.

Love. Oh! perfectly, Sir; they gratify my tafte of all things. One fees villas where nature reigns in a wild kind of fimplicity; but then they have no appearance of art, no art at all.

Drug. Very true, rightly diftinguifhed :----now mine is all art; no wild nature here; I did it all myfelf.

Love. What, had you none of the great proficients in gardening to affift you?

Drug. Lackaday! no,---ha! ha! I underftand thefe things---I love my garden. The front of my houfe, Mr. Lovelace, is not that very pretty?

Love.

Love. Elegant to a degree!

Drug. Don't you like the fun-dial, plac'd juſt by my dining-room windows?

Love. A perfect beauty!

Drug. I knew you'd like it---and the motto is ſo well adapted---*Tempus edax & index rerum*. And I know the meaning of it----Time eateth and diſcovereth all things---ha! ha! pretty, Mr. Lovelace! ---I have ſeen people ſo ſtare at it as they paſs by---ha! ha!

Love. Why now, I don't believe there's a nobleman in the kingdom has ſuch a thing.

Drug. Oh no----they have got into a falſe taſte. I bought that bit of ground the other ſide of the road---and it looks very pretty---I made a duck-pond there, for the ſake of the proſpect.

Love. Charmingly imagin'd!

Drug. My leaden images are well---

Love. They exceed ancient ſtatuary.

Drug. I love to be ſurpriz'd at the turning of a walk with an inanimate figure, that looks you full in the face, and can ſay nothing to you, while one is enjoying one's own thoughts----ha! ha!----Mr. Lovelace, I'll point out a beauty to you---Juſt by the haw-haw, at the end of my ground, there is a fine Dutch figure, with a ſcythe in his hand, and a pipe in his mouth---that's a jewel, Mr. Lovelace.

Love. That eſcap'd me: a thouſand thanks for pointing it out---I obſerve you have two very fine yew-trees before the houſe.

Drug. Lackaday, Sir! they look uncouth----I have a deſign about them---I intend---ha! ha! it will be very pretty, Mr. Lovelace---I intend to have them cut into the ſhape of the two giants at Guildhall---ha! ha!

Love. Exquifite!---why then they won't look like trees.

Drug. Oh, no, no----not at all----I won't have any thing in my garden that looks like what it is--- ha! ha!

Love. Nobody underftands thefe things like you, Mr. Drugget.

Drug. Lackaday! its all my delight now----this is what I have been working for. I have a great improvement to make ftill---I propofe to have my evergreens cut into fortifications, and then I fhall have the Moro caftle, and the Havanna; and then near it fhall be fhips of myrtle, failing upon feas of box to attack the town: won't that make my place look very rural, Mr. Lovelace?

Love. Why you have the moft fertile invention, Mr. Drugget.

Drug. Ha! ha! this is what I have been work-ing for. I love my garden---but I muft beg your pardon for a few moments---I muft ftep and fpeak with a famous nurfery-man, who is come to offer me fome choice things.---Do go and join the com-pany, Mr. Lovelace---my daughter Rackett and Sir Charles will be here prefently---I fhan't go to bed till I fee 'em---ha! ha!---my place is prettily variegated---this is what I have been working for ---I fin'd for Sheriff to enjoy thefe things---ha! ha!
[*Exit.*

Love. Poor Mr. Drugget! Mynheer Van Thun-dertentrunck, in his little box at the fide of a dyke, has as much tafte and elegance.---However, if I can but carry off his daughter, if I can but rob his garden of that flower----why then I fhall fay, " This is what I have been working for."

I

3

Woodley
Druggit
M.ª Druggit

Enter Dimity.

Dim. Do lend us your affiftance, Mr. Lovelace
---you're a fweet gentleman, and love a good na-
tur'd action.

Love. Why how now! what's the matter?

Dim. My 'mafter is going to cut the two yew-
trees into the fhape of two devils, I believe; and
my poor miftrefs is breaking her heart for it.---Do,
run and advife him againft it---fhe is your friend,
you know fhe is, Sir.

Love. Oh, if that's all---I'll make that matter eafy
directly.

Dim. My miftrefs will be for ever oblig'd to
you; and you'll marry her daughter in the morning.

Love. Oh, my rhetoric fhall diffuade him.

Dim. And, Sir, put him againft dealing with that
nurfery-man; Mrs. Drugget hates him.

Love. Does fhe?

Dim. Mortally.

Love. Say no more, the bufinefs is done. [*Exit.*

Dim. If he fays one word, old Drugget will never
forgive him.---My brain was at its laft fhift; but if
this plot takes---So, here comes our Nancy.

Enter Nancy. *R.H*

Nan. Well, Dimity, what's to become of me?

Dim. My ftars! what makes you up, Mifs?----I
thought you were gone to bed!

Nan. What fhould I go to bed for? Only to tum-
ble and tofs, and fret, and be uneafy---they are going
to marry me, and I am frighted out of my wits.

Dim. Why then, you're the only young lady
within fifty miles round, that would be frighten'd
at fuch a thing.

Nan. Ah! if they would let me chufe for myfelf.

　　　　　　　　　　　　　　　　　Dim.

Dim. Don't you like Mr. Lovelace?

Nan. My mama does, but I don't; I don't mind his being a man of fashion, not I.

Dim. And, pray, can you do better than follow the fashion?

Nan. ~~Ah! I know there's a fashion for new bon-nets, and a fashion for dressing the hair-ribbon;~~ I never heard of a fashion for the heart. *Dimity.*

Dim. Why then, my dear, the heart moftly follows the fashion now.

Nan. Does it!---pray who fets the fashion of the heart?

Dim. All the fine ladies in London, o'my con-fcience.

Nan. And what's the laft new fashion, pray?

Dim. Why, to marry any fop that has a few de-ceitful agreeable appearances about him; fomething of a pert phrafe, a good operator for the teeth, and tolerable taylor.

Nan. And do they marry without loving?

Dim. Oh! marrying for love has been a great while out of fashion.

Nan. Why, then I'll wait till that fashion comes up again.

Dim. And then, Mr. Lovelace, I reckon—

Nan. Pfhaw! I don't like him; he talks to me as if he was the moft miferable man in the world, and the confident thing looks fo pleas'd with himfelf all the while.----I want to marry for love, and not for card-playing---I fhould not be able to bear the life my fifter leads with Sir Charles Rackett---and I'll forfeit my ~~new cap,~~ if they don't quarrel foon. *life*

Dim. Oh fie! no! they won't quarrel yet a-while.----A quarrel in three weeks after marriage, would be fomewhat of the quickeft---By and by we fhall hear of their whims and their humours---Well, but

but if you don't like Mr. Lovelace, what fay you
to Mr. Woodley?

Nan. Ah!---I don't know what to fay---but I
can fing fomething that will explain my mind.

S O N G.

WHEN firft the dear youth paffing by,
  Difclos'd his fair form to my fight,
I gaz'd, but I could not tell why;
  My heart it went throb with delight.

As nearer he drew, thofe fweet eyes
  Were with their dear meaning fo bright,
I trembled, and loft in furprize,
  My heart it went throb with delight.

When his lips their dear accents did try
  The return of my love to excite,
I feign'd, yet began to guefs why
  My heart it went throb with delight.

We chang'd the ftol'n glance, the fond fmile,
  Which lovers alone read aright;
We look'd, and we figh'd, yet the while
  Our hearts they went throb with delight.

Confent I foon blufh'd, with a figh,
  My promife I ventur'd to plight;
Come, Hymen, we then fhall know why
  Our hearts they go throb with delight.

Re-Enter Woodley.

Wood. My fweeteft angel! I have heard all, and
my heart overflows with love and gratitude.

Nan. Ah! but I did not know you was liftening.
You fhould not have betray'd me fo, Dimity: I
fhall be angry with you.

C   *Dim.*

Dim. Well, I'll take my chance for that.---Run both into my room, and fay all your pretty things to one another there, for here comes the old gentleman---make hafte away.

[*Exeunt* Woodley *and* Nancy. *ML*

Act Drugget

Enter Drugget. *LH*

Drug. A forward prefuming coxcomb!---Dimity, do you ftep to Mrs. Drugget, and fend her hither.

Dim. Yes, Sir;---~~It works upon him, I fee~~. [*Exit. R*

Drug. The yew-trees ought not to be cut, becaufe they'll help to keep off the duft, and I am too near the road already---a forry ignorant fop !---When I am in fo fine a fituation, and can fee every carriage that goes by.----And then to abufe the nurfery-man's rarities !---A finer fucking pig in lavender, with fage growing in his belly, was never feen !---And yet he wants me not to have it----But have it I will.----- There's a fine tree of Knowledge, too, with Adam and Eve in juniper; Eve's nofe not quite grown, but it's thought in the fpring will be very forward--- I'll have that too, with the ferpent in ground ivy--- two poets in wormwood---I'll have them both. Ay; and there's a Lord Mayor's feaft in honeyfuckle; and the whole court of Aldermen in hornbeam ~~; and three modern beaux in jeffamine, fomewhat ftunted: they all fhall be in my garden~~, with the Dragon of Wantley in box---all---all---I'll have 'em all, let my wife and Mr. Lovelace fay what they will---

Dimity

Sir Char.

Enter Mrs. Drugget. *RH*

Mrs. D. Did you fend for me, lovey ?

Drug. The yew-trees fhall be cut into the giants of Guildhall, whether you will or not.

Mrs. D. Sure my own dear will do as he pleafes.

Drug. And the pond, tho' you praife the green
banks,

banks, fhall be wall'd round, and I'll have a little fat boy in marble, fpouting up water in the middle.

Mrs. D. My fweet, who hinders you?

Drug. Yes, and I'll buy the nurfery-man's whole catalogue---Do you think, after retiring to live all the way here, almoft four miles from London, that I won't do as I pleafe in my own garden.

Mrs. D. My dear, but why are you in fuch a paffion?

Drug. I'll have the lavender pig, and the Adam and Eve, and the Dragon of Wantley, and all of 'em---and there fhan't be a more romantic fpot on the London road than mine.

Mrs. D. I'm fure it's as pretty as hands can make it.

Drug. I did it all myfelf, and I'll do more---- And Mr. Lovelace fhan't have my daughter.

Mrs. D. No! what's the matter now, Mr. Drugget?

Drug. He fhall learn better manners than to abufe my houfe and gardens.---You put him in the head of it, but I'll difappoint ye both---And fo you may go and tell Mr. Lovelace that the match is quite off.

Mrs. D. I can't comprehend all this, not I,--- but I'll tell him fo, if you pleafe, my dear---I am willing to give myfelf pain, if it will give you pleafure: muft I give myfelf pain?---Don't afk me, pray don't;---I don't like pain.

Drug. I am refolv'd, and it fhall be fo.

Mrs. D. Let it be fo then. (*cries*) Oh! oh! cruel man! I fhall break my heart if the match is broke off---if it is not concluded to-morrow, fend for an undertaker, and bury me the next day.

Drug. How! I don't want that neither—

Mrs. D. Oh! oh!—

Drug.

Drug. I am your lord and mafter, my dear, but not your executioner---Before George, it muft never be faid that my wife died of too much compliance ---Chear up, my love------and this affair fhall be fettled as foon as Sir Charles and Lady Rackett arrive.

Mrs. D. You bring me to life again------You know, my fweet, what an happy couple Sir Charles and his lady are------Why fhould not we make our Nancy as happy?

Enter Dimity.

Dim. Sir Charles and his lady, Ma'am.

Mrs. D. Oh! charming! I'm tranfported with joy---Where are they? I long to fee 'em?   [*Exit.*

Dim. Well, Sir; the happy couple are arriv'd.

Drug. Yes, they do live happy indeed.

Dim. But how long will it laft?

Drug. How long! don't forbode any ill, you jade---don't, I fay---It will laft during their lives, I hope.

Dim. Well, mark the end of it---Sir Charles, I know, is gay and good-humour'd---but he can't bear the leaft contradiction, no, not in the mereft trifle.

Drug. Hold your tongue---hold your tongue.

Dim. Yes, Sir, I have done;---and yet there is in the compofition of Sir Charles a certain humour, which, like the flying gout, gives no difturbance to the family till it fettles in the head---When once it fixes there, mercy on every body about him! but here he comes.   [*Exit.*

Enter Sir Charles.

Sir Cha. My dear Sir, I kifs your hand---but why ftand on ceremony? To find you up thus late, mortifies me beyond expreffion.   *Drug.*

Drug. 'Tis but once in a way, Sir Charles.

Sir Cha. My obligations to you are inexpreſſible ; you have given me the moſt amiable of girls ; our tempers accord like uniſons in muſic.

Drug. Ah ! that's what makes me happy in my old days ; my children and my garden are all my care.

Sir Cha. And my friend Lovelace---he is to have our ſiſter Nancy, I find.

Drug. Why my wife is ſo minded.

Sir Cha. Oh, by all means, let her be made happy ---A very pretty fellow Lovelace----And as to that Mr.---Woodley I think you call him---he is but a plain underbred, ill faſhioned ſort of a---nobody knows him ; he is not one of us---Oh, by all means marry her to one of us.

Drug. I believe it muſt be ſo---Would you take any refreſhment ?

Sir Cha. Nothing in nature—it is time to retire.

Drug. Well, well ! good night then, Sir Charles —Ha ! here comes my daughter—Good night, Sir Charles.

Sir Cha. Bon repos.

Drug. (*going out*) My Lady Rackett, I'm glad to hear how happy you are, I won't detain you now —there's your good man waiting for you—good night, my girl. [*Exit.*

Sir Cha. I muſt humour this old putt, in order to be remember'd in his will.

Enter Lady Rackett.

Lady R. O la !—I'm quite fatigu'd—I can hardly move—why don't you help me, you barbarous man ?

Sir Cha. There ; take my arm—" Was ever thing ſo pretty made to walk."

Lady

Lady R. But I won't be laugh'd at—I don't love you.

Sir Cha. Don't you?

Lady R. No. Dear me! this glove! why don't you help me off with my glove! pſhaw!——You aukward thing, let it alone; you an't fit to be about me, I might as well not be married, for any uſe you are of—reach me a chair—you have no com-paſſion for me—I am ſo glad to ſit down—why do you drag me to routs—You know I hate 'em?

Sir Cha. Oh! there's no exiſting, no breathing, unleſs one does as other people of faſhion do.

Lady R. But I'm out of humour, I loſt all my money.

Sir Cha. How much?

Lady R. Three hundred.

Sir Cha. Never fret for that—I don't value three hundred pounds to contribute to your happineſs.

Lady R. Don't you?—Not value three hundred pounds to pleaſe me?

Sir Cha. You know I don't.

Lady R. Ah! you fond fool!——But I hate gaming---It almoſt metamorphoſes a woman into a fury——Do you know that I was frighted at myſelf ſeveral times to-night——I had an huge oath at the very tip of my tongue.

Sir Cha. Had ye?

Lady R. I caught myſelf at it---and ſo I bit my lips——and then I was cramm'd up in a corner of the room with ſuch a ſtrange party at a whiſt-table, looking at black and red ſpots---did you mind 'em?

Sir Cha. You know I was buſy elſewhere.

Lady R. There was that ſtrange unaccountable woman, Mrs. Nightſhade---She behav'd ſo ſtrangely to her huſband, a poor, inoffenſive, good-natur'd, good ſort of a good for nothing kind of man,——

but

but fhe fo teiz'd him---" How could you play that card? Ah, youv'e a head, and fo has a pin——You're a numfcull, you know you are——Ma'am, he has the pooreft head in the world, he does not know what he is about; you know you don't---Ah fye! I'm afham'd of you!"

Sir Cha. She has ferv'd to divert you, I fee..

Lady R. And then, to crown all---there was my Lady Clackit, who runs on with an eternal volubility of nothing, out of all feafon, time, and place ---In the very mid'ft of the game fhe begins,——" Lard, Ma'am, I was apprehenfive I fhould not be able to wait on your La'fhip---my poor little dog, Pompey---the fweeteft thing in the world,---a fpade led!---there's the knave---I was fetching a walk, Me'm, the other morning in the Park---a fine frofty morning it was---I love frofty weather of all things---let me look at the laft trick---and fo, M'em, little Pompey---and if your La'fhip was to fee the dear creature pinch'd with the froft, and mincing his fteps along the Mall---with his pretty little innocent face---I vow I don't know what to play---and fo, Me'm, while I was talking to Captain Flimfey---Your La'fhip knows Captain Flimfey---Nothing but rubbifh in my hand---I can't help it ---and fo, Me'm, five odious frights of dogs befet my poor little Pompey---the dear creature has the heart of a lion, but who can refift five at once?---And fo Pompey barked for affiftance---the hurt he received was upon his cheft---the doctor would not advife him to venture out till the wound is heal'd, for fear of an inflamation.---Pray what's trumps?

Sir Cha. My dear, you'd make a moft excellent actrefs.

Lady R. Well, now let's go to reft---but Sir Charles, how fhockingly you play'd that laft rubber, when I ftood looking over you!

Sir Cha.

Sir Cha. My love, I play'd the truth of the game.

Lady R. No, indeed, my dear, you play'd it wrong.

Sir Cha. Po! nonfenfe! you don't underftand it.

Lady R. I beg your pardon, I'm allowed to play better than you.

Sir Cha. All conceit, my dear, I was perfectly right.

Lady R. No fuch thing, Sir Charles, the diamond was the play.

Sir Cha. Po! po! ridiculous! the club was the card againft the world.

Lady R. Oh! no, no, no, I fay it was the diamond.

Sir Cha. Zounds! Madam, I fay it was the club.

Lady R: What do you fly into fuch a paffion for?

Sir Cha. 'Sdeath and fury, do you think I don't know what I'm about? I tell you once more, the club was the judgment of it.

Lady R. May be fo---have it your own way. (*walks about and fings*)

Sir Cha. Vexation! you're the ftrangeft woman that ever liv'd; there's no converfing with you--- Look'ye here, my Lady Rackett---it's the cleareft cafe in the world, I'll make it plain in a moment.

Lady R. Well, Sir! ha! ha! ha! (*with a fneering laugh*)

Sir Cha. I had four cards left---a trump was led ---they were fix---no, no, no, they were feven, and we nine---then you know---the beauty of the play was to---

Lady R. Well, now it's amazing to me, that you can't fee it---give me leave, Sir Charles---your left hand adverfary had led his laft trump---and he had before finefs'd the club, and rough'd the diamond ---now if you had put on your diamond---

Sir Cha.

∧ but you did not get it.

Sir Cha. Zoons! Madam, but we play'd for the odd trick. *I know you play'd for this odd trick*

Lady R. ~~And sure the play for the odd trick~~---

Sir Cha. Death and fury I can't you hear me?

Lady R. Go on, Sir.

Sir Cha. Zoons! hear me, I say,---Will you hear me?

Lady R. I never heard the like in my life. [*Hums a tune, and walks about fretfully*]

Sir Cha. Why then you are enough to provoke the patience of a Stoick.---[*looks at her, and she walks about, and laughs uneasily*] Very well, Madam; ---You know no more of the game than your father's leaden Hercules on the top of the house--- You know no more of whist than he does of gardening.

Lady R. Ha! ha! ha! [*Takes out a glass and settles her hair*]

Sir Cha. You're a vile woman, and I'll not sleep another night under one roof with you.

Lady R. As you please, Sir.

Sir Cha. Madam, it shall be as I please---I'll order my chariot this moment---[*Going.*] I know how the cards should be play'd as well as any man in England, that let me tell you---[*Going*]---And when your family were standing behind counters, measuring out tape, and bartering for Whitechapel needles, my ancestors, my ancestors, Madam, were squandering away whole estates at cards; whole estates, my Lady Rackett---[*she hums a tune, and he looks at her*]---Why then, by all that's dear to me, I'll never exchange another word with you, good, bad, or indifferent---Look'ye, my Lady Rackett---thus it stood---the trump being led, it was then my business---

Lady R. To play the diamond, to be sure.

D   *Sir Cha.*

Sir Cha. 'Damn it, I have done with you for ever, and so you may tell your father.   [*Exit.* ℞

Lady R. What a passion the gentleman's in! ha! ha! [*laughs in a peevish manner*] I promise him, I'll not give up my judgment.

Re- *Enter* Sir Charles.

Sir Cha. My Lady Rackett, look'ye, Ma'am--- once more, out of pure good-nature---

Lady R. Sir, I am convinc'd of your good-nature.

Sir Cha. That, and that only prevails with me to tell you, the club was the play.

Lady R. Well, be it so---I have no objection.

Sir Cha. It's the clearest point in the world--- we were nine, and—

Lady R. And for that very reason :---You know the club was the best in the house.

Sir Cha. There is no such thing as talking to you ---You're a base woman---I'll part from you for ever; you may live here with your father, and admire his fantastical evergreens, till you grow as fantastical yourself---I'll set out for London this instant---[*stops at the door.*] The club was not the best in the house.

Lady R. How calm you are? Well!---I'll go to bed;---will you come?---You had better--- come then---you shall come to bed---not come to bed when I ask you!---Poor Sir Charles! [*looks and laughs, then exit.* L.D

Sir Cha. That ease is provoking. [*crosses to the opposite door where she went out*]---I tell you the dia- mond was not the play, and I here take my final leave of you---[*Walks back as fast as he can*] I am resolv'd upon it, and I know the club was not the best in the house.   [*Exit.* ℞

ACT

ACT II.

Scene Continues *Enter* Dimity.

Dimity.

HA! ha! ah! oh! Heavens! I fhall expire in a fit of laughing---this is the modifh couple that were fo happy---fuch a quarrel as they have had---the whole houfe is in an uproar---ha! ha! ~~a rare proof of the happinefs they enjoy in high life. I fhall never think people of fafhion mentioned again, but I fhall be ready to die in a fit of laughter.~~ ---ho! ho! ho! this is three weeks after marriage, I think.

Enter Drugget.

Drug. Hey! how! what's the matter, Dimity? ---What am I call'd down ftairs for?

Dim Why, there's two people of fafhion---- [*ftifles a laugh*]

Drug. Why, you faucy minx!---Explain this moment.

Dim. The fond couple have been together by-the ears this half hour---are you fatisfied now?

Drug. Ay!---what have they quarrell'd---what was it about?

Dim. Something above my comprehenfion, and yours too, I believe---People in high life under-ftand their own forms beft---And here comes one that can unriddle the whole affair. [*Exit.*

Enter Sir Charles.

Sir Cha. [*To the people within*] I fay, let the horfes be put-to this moment---So, Mr. Drugget.

Drug.

Drug. Sir Charles, here's a terrible buſtle---I did not expect this---what can be the matter?

Sir Cha. I have been us'd by your daughter in ſo baſe, ſo contemptuous a manner, that I am deter-mined not to ſtay in this houſe to-night.

Drug. This is a thunder-bolt to me! after ſeeing how elegantly and faſhionably you liv'd together, to find now all ſunſhine vaniſh'd---Do, Sir Charles, let me heal this breach, if poſſible.

Sir Cha. Sir, 'tis impoſſible---I'll not live with her a day longer.

Drug. Nay, nay, don't be over haſty.---let me intreat you, go to bed and ſleep upon it---in the morning, when you're cool---

Sir Cha. Oh, Sir, I am very cool, I aſſure---ha! ha!---it is not in her power, Sir, to---a---a---to diſturb the ſerenity of my temper---Don't imagine that I'm in a paſſion---I'm not ſo eaſily ruffled as you may imagine---But quietly and deliberately I can repay the injuries done me by a falſe, ungrate-ful, deceitful wife.

Drug. The injuries done you by a falſe, ungrate-ful wife! my daughter, I hope---

Sir Cha. Her character is now fully known to me ---ſhe's a vile woman! that's all I have to ſay, Sir.

Drug. Hey! how!---a vile woman---what has ſhe done---I hope ſhe is not capable---

Sir Cha. I ſhall enter into no detail, Mr. Drug-get; the time and circumſtances won't allow it at preſent------But depend upon it, I have done with her------a low, unpoliſh'd, uneducated, falſe, im-poſing------See if the horſes are put-to.

Drug. Mercy on me! in my old days to hear this,

Enter Mrs. Drugget. *S.H*

Mrs. D. Deliver me! I am all over in ſuch a tremble

$\triangle$

2.

Ld Rackett
Mrs Drugget
Dimity

tremble——Sir Charles, I shall break my heart if
there's any thing amiss.

Sir Cha. Madam, I am very sorry, for your fake
——but there is no possibility of living with her.

Mrs. D. My poor dear girl! What can she have
done?

Sir Cha. What all her fex can do, the very spirit
of them all.

Drug. Ay! ay! ay!—She's bringing foul dif-
grace upon us——This comes of her marrying a
man of fashion.

Sir Cha. Fashion, Sir!---that should have in-
structed her better---she might have been sensible
of her happiness—Whatever you may think of the
fortune you gave her, my rank in life claims respect
---claims obedience, attention, truth, and love, from
one raised in the world, as she has been by an
alliance with me.

Drug. And let me tell you, however you may
estimate your quality, my daughter is dear to me.

Sir Cha. And, Sir, my character is dear to me.

Drug. Yes you must give me leave to tell you—

Sir Cha. I won't hear a word.

Drug. Not in behalf of my own daughter?

Sir Cha. Nothing can excuse her—'tis to no purpofe—she has married above her; and if that cir-
cumstance makes the lady forget herself, she at least
shall fee that I can, and will support my own dignity.

Drug. But, Sir, I have a right to ask—

Mrs. D. Patience, my dear, be a little calm.

Drug. Mrs. Drugget, do you have patience, I
must and will enquire.

Mrs. D. Don't be fo hasty, my love; have fome
respect for Sir Charles's rank; don't be violent with
a man of his fashion.

Drug. Hold your tongue, woman, I fay——
you're

you're not a perfon of fafhion at leaft——My
daughter was ever a good girl.

Sir Cha. I have found her out.

Drug. Oh! then it is all over—and it does not
fignify arguing about it.

Mrs. D. That ever I fhould live to fee this hour!
how the unfortunate girl could take fuch wickednefs
in her head, I can't imagine—I'll go and fpeak to
the unhappy creature this moment.   [*Exit.* *L.H*

Sir Cha. She ftands detected now—detected in
her trueft colours.

Drug. Well, grievous as it may be, let me hear
the circumftances of this unhappy bufinefs.

Sir Cha. Mr. Drugget, I have not leifure now—
but her behaviour has been fo exafperating, that I
fhall make the beft of my way to town—My mind
is fixed—She fees me no more, and fo, your fer-
vant, Sir.   [*Exit.*

Drug. What a calamity has here befallen us! a
good girl, and fo well difpos'd, till the evil com-
munication of high life, and fafhionable vices,
turn'd her to folly.

Enter Lovelace.

Love. Joy! joy! Mr. Drugget, I give you joy.

Drug. Don't infult me, Sir!—I defire you wont.

Love. Infult you, Sir!——is there any thing in-
fulting, my dear Sir, if I take the liberty to con-
gratulate you on---

Drug. There! there!---the manners of high life
for you---he thinks there's nothing in all this——
the ill behaviour of a wife he thinks an ornament to
her character---Mr. Lovelace, you fhall have no
daughter of mine.

Love. My dear Sir, never bear malice---I have
reconfidered the thing, and curfe catch me, if I

don't

Song — Sir Charles Sir Charles I beg
you will hear me

follow Sir Charles

don't think your notion of the Guildhall giants, and
the court of Aldermen in hornbeam---

Drug. Well! well! well! there may be people
at the court end of the town in hornbeam too.

Love. Yes, faith, so there may---and I believe
I could recommend you to a tolerable collection---
however, with your daughter I am ready to venture.

Drug. But I am not ready---I'll not venture my
girl with you---no more daughters of mine shall
have their minds deprav'd by polite vices.

Enter Woodley.

Mr. Woodley---you shall have Nancy to your wife,
as I promis'd you---take her to-morrow morning.

Wood. Sir, I have not words to exprefs---

Love. What the devil is the matter with the old
haberdafher now?

Drug. And hark ye, Mr. Woodley---I'll make
you a prefent for your garden, of a coronation
dinner in greens, with a champion riding on horfe-
back, and the fword will be full grown before April
next.

Wood. I shall receive it, Sir, as your favour.

Drug. Ay, ay! I fee my error in wanting an
alliance with great folks---I had rather have you,
Mr. Woodley, for my fon-in-law, than any courtly
fop of 'em all. Is this man gone?---Is Sir Charles
Rackett gone?

Wood. Not yet;---he makes a bawling yonder for
his horfe---I'll ftep and call him to you. [*Exit.*

Drug. I am out of all patience---I am out of my
fenfes---I muft fee him once more---Mr. Lovelace,
neither you nor any perfon of fafhion, shall ruin
another daughter of mine. [*Exit.*

Love. Droll this! damn'd droll! and every fyl-
lable of it Arabic to me---the queer old putt is as

whimfical

whimſical in his notions of life as of gardening. If
this be the caſe---I'll bruſh, and leave him to his
devotion. [*Exit.*

Enter Lady Rackett, Mrs. Drugget, *and* Dimity.

Lady R. A cruel, barbarous man! to quarrel in
this unaccountable manner; to alarm the whole
houſe, and expoſe me and himſelf too.

Mrs. D. Oh, child! I never thought it would
have come to this---your ſhame won't end here! it
will be all over St. James's pariſh by to-morrow
morning.

Lady R. Well, if it muſt be ſo, there's one comfort, the ſtory will tell more to his diſgrace than
mine.

Dim. As I'm a ſinner, and ſo it will, Madam.
He deſerves what he has met with, I think.

Mrs. D. Dimity, don't you encourage her---you
ſhock me to hear you ſpeak ſo---I did not think
you had been ſo harden'd.

Lady R. Harden'd do you call it?---I have liv'd
in the world to very little purpoſe, if ſuch trifles as
theſe are to diſturb my reſt.

Mrs. D. You wicked girl!---Do you call it a
trifle to be guilty of falſhood to your huſband's bed?

Lady R. How!---[*Turns ſhort and ſtares at her.*

Dim. That! that's a mere trifle indeed---I have
been in as good places as any body, and not a
creature minds it now, I'm ſure.

Mrs. D. My Lady Rackett, my Lady Rackett,
I never could think to ſee you come to this deplo-
rable ſhame.

Lady R. Surely the baſe man has not been capable
of laying any thing of that ſort to my charge---
[*Aſide*] All this is unaccountable to me---ha! ha!
'tis ridiculous beyond meaſure.

Dim.

5th

$$\frac{3}{}$$

Sir charles
Snigget

Dim. That's right, Madam.——Laugh at it——you ferv'd him right.

Mrs. D. Charlotte! Charlotte! I'm aftonifh'd at your wickednefs.

Lady R. Well, I proteft and vow I don't comprehend all this——has Sir Charles accus'd me of any impropriety in my conduct?

Mrs. D. Oh! too true, he has——he has found you out, and you have behav'd bafely, he fays.

Lady R. Madam!

Mrs. D. You have fallen into frailty, like many others of your fex, he fays; and he is refolv'd to come to a feperation directly.

Lady R. Why then, if he is fo bafe a wretch as to difhonour me in that manner, his heart fhall ake before I live with him again. ——— *Exit L. H*

Dim. Hold to that, Ma'am, and let his head ake into the bargain.

Mrs. D. Your poor father heard it as well as me.

Lady R. Then let your doors be open'd for him this very moment——let him return to London——if he does not, I'll lock myfelf up, and the falfe one fhan't approach me, tho' he beg on his knees at my very door——a bafe injurious man! *[Exit. L. H*

Mrs. D. Dimity, do let us follow, and hear what fhe has to fay for herfelf. *[Exit. L. H*

Dim. She has excufe enough, I warrant her—— What a noife is here indeed!——I have liv'd in polite families, where there was no fuch buftle made about nothing. *[Exit. L. H*

Scene 2. *Enter* Sir Charles *and* Drugget. *R. H*

Sir Cha. 'Tis in vain, Sir, my refolution is taken——

Drug. Well, but confider, I am her father—— indulge me only till we hear what the girl has to fay in her defence.

E   *Sir*

Sir Cha. She can have nothing to fay——no excufe can palliate fuch behaviour.

Drug. Don't be too pofitive---there may be fome miftake.

Sir Cha. No miftake--did not I fee her, hear her myfelf?

Drug. Lackaday! then I am an unfortunate man!

Sir Cha. She will be unfortunate too---with all my heart---fhe may thank herfelf---fhe might have been happy, had fhe been fo difpos'd.

Drug. Why truly, I think fhe might.

Enter Mrs. Drugget. *L.H*

Mrs. D. I wifh you'd moderate your anger a little---and let us talk over this affair with temper--- my daughter denies every tittle of your charge.

Sir Cha. Denies it! denies it!

Mrs. D. She does indeed.

Sir Cha. And that aggravates her fault.

Mrs. D. She vows you never found her out in any thing that was wrong.

Sir Cha. So! fhe does not allow it to be wrong then!——Madam, I tell you again, I know her thoroughly, I fay, I have found her out, and I am now acquainted with her character.

Mrs. D. Then you are in oppofite ftories—— fhe fwears, my dear Mr. Drugget, the poor girl fwears fhe never was guilty of the fmalleft infidelity to her hufband in her born days.

Sir Cha. And what then?---What if fhe does fay fo!

Mrs. D. And if fhe fays truly, it is hard her cha- racter fhould be blown upon without juft caufe.

Sir Cha. And is fhe therefore to behave ill in other refpects? I never charg'd her with infidelity to me, Madam---there I allow her innocent.

Drug.

Drug. And did not you charge her then ?

Sir Cha. No, Sir, I never dreamt of such a thing.

Drug. Why then, if she's innocent, let me tell you, you're a scandalous person.

Mrs. D. Prithee, my dear---

Drug. Be quiet---tho' he is a man of quality, I will tell him of it---did not I fine for sheriff?---Yes, you are a scandalous person to defame an honest man's daughter.

Sir Cha. What have you taken into your head now ?

Drug. You charg'd her with falshood to your bed.

Sir Cha. No---never---never.

Drug. But I say you did---you call'd yourself a cuckold---did not he, wife ?

Mrs. D. Yes, lovey, I'm witness.

Sir Cha. Absurd ! I said no such thing.

Drug. But I aver you did.

Mrs. D. You did, indeed, Sir.

Sir Cha. But I tell you no---positively no.

Drug. and Mrs. D. And I say yes, positively yes---

Sir Cha. 'Sdeath, this is all madness---

Drug. You said she follow'd the ways of most of her sex.

Sir Cha. I said so---and what then ?

Drug. There he owns it---owns that he call'd himself a cuckold---and without rhyme or reason into the bargain.

Sir Cha. I never own'd any such thing.

Drug. You own'd it even now---now---now---now.

Enter Dimity, *in a fit of laughing.*

Dim. What do you think it was all about---ha ! ha ! the whole secret is come out, ha ! ha !---It was all about a game of cards---ha ! ha !---

Drug.

Drug. A game of cards !

Dim. (laughing) It was all about a club and a diamond. *(runs out laughing)— Exit L. H*

Drug. And was that all, Sir Charles ?

Sir Cha. And enough too, Sir---

Drug. And was that what you found her out in !

Sir Cha. I can't bear to be contradicted when I'm clear that I'm in the right.

Drug. I never heard such a heap of nonsense in all my life---Woodley shall marry Nancy.

Mrs. D. Don't be in a hurry, my love, this will all be made up.

Drug. Why does not he go and beg her pardon, then ?

Sir Cha. I beg her pardon ! I won't debase myself to any of you---I shan't forgive her you may rest affur'd. [*Exit. H.*

Drug. Now there---there's a pretty fellow for you.

Mrs. D. I'll step and prevail on my Lady Rackett to speak to him---then all will be well. [*Exit. L.*

Drug. A ridiculous fop ! I'm glad its no worse, however.

Enter Nancy. *L. H*

So Nancy---you seem in confusion, my girl !

Nan. How can one help it ?---With all this noise in the house, and you're going to marry me as ill as my sister---I hate Mr. Lovelace.

Drug. Why so, child ?

Nan. I know these people of quality despise us all out of pride, and would be glad to marry us out of avarice.

Drug. The girl's right.

Nan. They marry one woman, live with another, and love only themselves.

Drug.

5

Sir Charles — Pack of Cards

Mrs Doggget

Candles —
&
Pack of Cards } on Table
2 Chairs

b
‾‾‾‾‾
Songget
L.d Rackett

Drug. And then quarrel about a card.

Nan. I don't want to be a gay lady---I want to be happy.

Drug. And fo you fhall---don't fright yourfelf, child---ftep to your fifter, bid her make herfelf eafy ---go, and comfort her, go.

Nan. Yes, Sir.   [*Exit.*

Drug. I'll ftep and fettle the matter with Mr. Woodley this moment.   [*Exit.*

Enter Sir Charles, *with a pack of cards in his hand.*

Sir Cha. Never was any thing like her behaviour ---I can pick out the very cards I had in my hand, and then 'tis as plain as the fun---there---now--- there---no---damn it---no---there it was---now let's fee---they had four by honours---and we play'd for the odd trick---damnation !---honours were divided ---ay ! honours were divided---and then a trump was led---and the other fide had the---confufion !--- this prepofterous woman has put it all out of my head---[*Puts the cards into his pocket.*] Mighty well, Madam; I have done with you.

Enter Mrs. Drugget.

Mrs. D. Come, Sir Charles, let me prevail------ Come with me and fpeak to her.

Sir Cha. I don't defire to fee her face.

Mrs. D. If you were to fee her all bath'd in tears, I am fure it would melt your very heart.

Sir Cha. Madam, it fhall be my fault if ever I am treated fo again---I'll have nothing to fay to her ---[*going, ftops*] Does fhe give up the point ?

Mrs. D. She does, fhe agrees to any thing.

Sir Cha. Does fhe allow that the club was the play?

Mrs. D. Juft as you pleafe---fhe's all fubmiffion.

                    Sir Cha.

Sir Cha. Does she own that the club was not the beft in the houfe?

Mrs. D. She does---fhe does.

Sir Cha. Then I'll ftep and fpeak to her——I *L.H* never was clearer in any thing in my life. [*Exit.*

Mrs. D. Lord love 'em, they'll make it up now ——and then they'll be as happy as ever. [*Enter Sing*

Enter Nancy.

Nan. Well! they may talk what they will of tafte, and genteel life——I don't think its natural ——Give me Mr. Woodley——La! there's that odious thing coming this way.

Enter Lovelace.

Love. My charming little innocent, I have not feen you thefe three hours.

Nan. I have been very happy thefe three hours.

Love. My fweet angel, you feem difconcerted--- And you neglect your pretty figure---No matter for the prefent; in a little time I fhall make you appear as graceful and genteel as your fifter.

Nan. That is not what employs my thoughts, Sir.

Love. Ay, but my pretty little dear, that fhou'd engage your attention——to fet off and adorn the charms that nature has given you, fhould be the bufinefs of your life.

Nan. Ah! but I have learnt a new fong that contradicts what you fay, and tho' I am not in a very good humour for finging, yet you fhall hear it.

Love. By all means;---don't check your fancy--- I am all attention.

Nan. It expreffes my fentiments, and when you have heard them, you won't teize me any more.

S O N G.

SONG.

To dance, and to drefs, and to flaunt it about,
To run to park, play, to affembly and rout,
To wander for ever in whim's giddy maze,
And one poor hair torture a million of ways:
To put, at the glafs, ev'ry feature to fchool,
And practife their art on each fop and each fool,
Of one thing to think, and another to tell,
Thefe, thefe are the manners of each giddy belle.

To fmile, and to fimper, white teeth to difplay;
The time in gay follies to trifle away;
Againft every virtue the bofom to fteel,
And only of drefs the anxieties feel;
To be at Eve's ear, the infiduous decoy,
The pleafure ne'er tafte, yet the mifchief enjoy,
To boaft of foft raptures they never can know,
Thefe, thefe are the manners of each giddy beau.

[*Exit.*

Love. I muft have her notwithftanding this——
for tho' I'm not in love, yet I'm in debt.

Enter Drugget.

Drug. So, ~~Mr. Lovelace~~ any news from above
ftairs? Is this abfurd quarrel at an end---Have they
made it up?

Love. Oh! ~~a mere bagatelle, Sir~~---thefe little
fracas among the better fort of people never laft
long--~~elegant trifles caufe elegant difputes, and we
come together elegantly again~~---as you fee---for
here they come, in perfect good-humour.

Enter Sir Charles *and* Lady Rackett.

Sir Cha. Mr. Drugget, I embrace you; Sir, you
fee me now in the moft perfect harmony of fpirits.

Drug.

Drug. What, all reconcil'd again?

Lady R. All made up, Sir---I knew how to bring him to my lure---This is the firſt difference, I think, we ever had, Sir Charles.

Sir Cha. And I'll be ſworn it ſhall be the laſt.

Drug. I am happy at laſt---Sir Charles, I can ſpare you an image to put on the top of your houſe in London.

Sir Cha. Infinitely oblig'd to you.

Drug. Well! well!---It's time to retire now---I am glad to ſee you reconciled---and now I'll wiſh you a good night, ~~Sir Charles. Mr. Lovelace, this is your way, and a very well done. I am glad your quarrels are at an end. This way, Mr. Lovelace.~~ [*Exeunt* ~~Lovelace and~~ *Drugget.*

Lady R. Ah! you're a ſad man, Sir Charles, to behave to me as you have done.

Sir Cha. My dear, I grant it---and ſuch an abſurd quarrel too---ha! ha!

~~Lady R. Yes---ha! ha!---about ſuch a trifle.~~

Sir Cha. It's pleaſant how we could both fall into ſuch an error---ha! ha!

~~Lady R. Ridiculous beyond expreſſion---ha! ha!~~

Sir Cha. And then the miſtake your father and mother fell into---ha! ha!

Lady R. That too is a diverting part of the ſtory—ha! ha!---But, Sir Charles, muſt I ſtay and live with my father till I grow as fantaſtical as his own evergreens.

Sir Cha. No, no, prithee---don't remind me of my folly.

Lady R. Ah! my relations were all ſtanding behind counters, ſelling Whitechapel needles, while your family were ſpending great eſtates.

Sir Cha. Nay, nay, ſpare my bluſhes.

Lady R.

i Charles take care of your lady — & I'll co
mfort ony old woman.
and Mrs Drugget — R.H

7
Servant with Slippers

A Sit down... sit down my dear—don't scream

Lady R. How could you fay fo harfh a thing? ---I don't love you,

Sir Cha. It was indelicate, I grant it.

Lady R. Am I a vile woman?

Sir Cha. How can you, my angel?

Lady R. I fhan't forgive you!---I'll have you on your knees for this. (*fings and plays with him*)--- " Go, naughty man."---Ah! Sir Charles!

Sir Cha. The reft of my life fhall aim at convincing you how fincerely I love---

Lady R. (*fings*) " Go, naughty man, I can't abide you."---Well! come let us go to reft. (*going*) Ah, Sir Charles!---now it is all over, the diamond was the play.

Sir Cha. Oh no, no, no,---my dear! ha! ha!--- it was the club indeed.

Lady R. Indeed, my love, you're miftaken. {*They sit*}

Sir Cha. Oh, no, no, no.

Lady R. But I fay, yes, yes, yes---[*Both laughing*]

Sir Cha. Pfhaw! no fuch thing---ha! ha!

Lady R. 'Tis fo, indeed---ha! ha!

Sir Cha. No, no, no---you'll make me die with laughing.

Lady R. Ay, and you make me laugh too--- ha! ha! (*toying with him*)

Enter Footman. *R.H.*

Footm. Your honour's cap and flippers.

Sir Cha. Ay, lay down my night-cap ---and here take thefe fhoes off [*he takes 'em off, and leaves 'em at a diftance*] Indeed my Lady Rackett, you make me ready to expire with laughing---ha! ha!

Lady R. You may laugh---but I'm right, notwith anding.

Sir Cha. How can you fay fo?

Lady R. How can you fay otherwife?

F *Sir Cha.*

Sir Cha. Well now mind me, my Lady Rackett
---We can now talk of this matter in good humour
---We can discuss it coolly.--- ~~let show will show~~

Lady R. So we can---and it's for that reason I
venture to speak to you---are these the ruffles I
bought for you?

Sir Cha. They are, my dear.

Lady R. They are very pretty---but indeed you
played the card wrong.

Sir Cha. Po, there is nothing so clear---if you
will but hear me---only hear me.

Lady R. Ah!---but do you hear me---the thing
was thus---the adversary's club being the best in
the house---

Sir Cha. How can you talk so!---[*somewhat
peevish*

Lady R. See there now---

Sir Cha. Listen to me---this was the affair---

Lady R. Pshaw! fiddlestick! hear me first.

Sir Cha. Po---no---damn it, let me speak.

Lady R. Well, to be sure you're a strange man.

Sir Cha. Plague and torture! there is no such
thing as conversing with you.

Lady R. ~~Very well, Sir! fly out again.~~

Sir Cha. Look here now ~~here's a pack of cards~~
·S· ---now you shall be convinc'd--- *here are the very*

Lady R. ~~You may talk till to-morrow, I know~~
I'm right. [*walks about*]

Sir Cha. Why then, ~~by all~~ that's perverse, you
~~are the most headstrong---Can't you look here now~~
~~here are the very~~ cards.

Lady R. Go on; you'll find it out at last.

Sir Cha. Damn it! will you let a man shew you. /\
~~Po! it's all nonsense---I'll talk no more about it~~
~~[puts up the cards] Come, we'll go to bed.~~

~~[going]~~

Mr Othn Dougget

~~Loose~~

Doodley Shandy

(He goes to the table) there are the very four
cards I held in my hands.

you see my love — those were my cards — it was
my lead — then I play'd that card —

Lady. — Yes, my love — I know you play'd
that card — but you should have play'd
that card.

[*going*] Now only ſtay a moment--- [*takes out the cards*] Now, mind me---ſee here---

Lady R. No, it does not ſignify---your head will be clearer in the morning---I'll go to bed.

Sir Cha. Stay a moment, can't ye.

Lady R. No---my head begins to ake---[affectedly]

Sir Cha. Why then, damn the cards---there---there [*throwing the cards about*] And there, and there---You may go to bed by yourſelf; and confuſion ſieze me, if I live a moment longer with you ---[*Putting on his ſhoes again*]

Enter Dimity.

Dim. Did you call, Sir?

Sir Cha. No, never, Madam.

Dim. (in a fit of laughing) What, at it again!

Lady R. Take your own way, Sir.

Sir Cha. Now then, I tell you once more you are a vile woman.

Dim. Law, Sir!---This is charming---I'll run and tell the old couple.   [*Exit.*

Sir Cha. (*ſtill putting on his ſhoes*) You are the moſt perverſe, obſtinate, nonſenſical---

Lady R. Ha! ha! don't make me laugh again, Sir Charles.

Sir Cha. Hell and the devil——Will you ſet down quietly, and let me convince you.

Lady R. I don't chuſe to hear any more about it.

Sir Cha. Why then I believe you are poſſeſſed---it is in vain to talk ſenſe and reaſon to you.

Lady R. Thank you for your compliment, Sir---ſuch a man [*with a ſneering laugh*] I never knew the like---[*ſits down*]

Sir Cha. I promiſe you, you ſhall repent of this uſage, before you have a moment of my company again---it ſhan't be in a hurry you may depend,

F 2   Madam

Lady Rackitt – Ha. ha. ha.

Madam. Now fee here—I can prove it to a demonstration [*fits down by her, fhe gets up*] Look ye there again now—you have the moft perverfe and peevifh temper'—I wifh I had never feen your face —I wifh I was a thoufand miles off from you—fit down but one moment.

Lady R. I'm difpos'd to walk about, Sir.

Sir Cha. Why then, may I perifh if ever,—a blockhead—an ideot I was to marry [*walks about*] fuch a provoking—impertinent—[*fhe fits down*] Damnation!—I am fo clear in the thing—fhe is not worth my notice---[*fits down, turns his back, and looks uneafy*] I'll take no more pains about it---[*Paufes for fome time, then looks at her*] Is not it very ftrange that you won't hear me?

Lady R. Sir, I am very ready to hear you.

Sir Cha. Very well then---very well---my dear ---you remember how the game ftood.

Lady R. I wifh you'd untie my necklace, it hurts me.

Sir Cha. Why can't you liften?

Lady R. I tell you it hurts me terribly.

Sir Cha. Death and confufion! there is no bearing this---you may be as wrong as you pleafe, and may I never hold four by honours, if I ever endeavour to fet you right again.   [*Exit.*

R H Enter Mr. *and* Mrs. Drugget, Woodley, Lovelace *and* Nancy. *L H*

Drug. What's here to do now?

Lady R. Never was fuch a man born---I did not fay a word to the gentleman---and yet he has been raving about the room like a madman.

Drug. And about a club again, I fuppofe.---Come hither, Nancy; Mr. Woodley, fhe is yours for life.

Mrs. D.

∧ In running off R H — he drives against
Mr. & Mrs. Dangget as they are entering

A: I wish he was put to bed with a spade

Mrs. D. My dear, how can you be-fo---

Drug. It fhall be fo---take her for life, Mr. Woodley.

Wood. My whole life fhall be devoted to her happinefs.

Love. The devil! and fo I am to be left in the lurch in this manner, am I?

Lady R. Oh! this is only one of thofe polite difputes which people of quality, who have nothing elfe to differ about, muft always be liable to---This will all be made up.

Drug. Never tell me---it's too late now---Mr. Woodley, I recommend my girl to your care---I fhall have nothing now to think of, but my greens, and my images, and my fhrubbery---though, mercy on all married folks, fay I! for thefe wranglings are, I am afraid, *What we muft all come to.*

Lady Rackett *coming forward.*

WHAT we muft all come to? *What?---Come to what?*

Muft broils and quarrels be the marriage lot?
If that's the wife, deep meaning of our poet,
The man's a fool! a blockhead! and I'll fhew it.
What could induce him in an age fo nice,
So fam'd for virtue, fo refin'd from vice,
To form a plan fo trivial, falfe, and low?
As if a belle could quarrel with a beau:
As if there were---in thefe thrice happy days,
One who from nature, or from reafon ftrays!
There's no crofs hufband now; no wrangling wife;
The man is downright ignorant of life.
'Tis the millennium this---devoid of guile,
Fair gentle truths, and white-rob'd candour fmile.

From

From every breast the sordid love of gold
Is banish'd quite---no boroughs now are sold!
Pray tell me, Sirs---[for I don't know I vow,]
Pray---is there such a thing as Gaming now?
Do peers make laws against that giant vice?
And then at Arthur's break them in a trice?
No---no---our lives are virtuous all, austere and hard;
Pray, Ladies---do you ever see a card?
Those empty boxes shew you don't love plays;
The managers, poor souls! get nothing now a days.
If here you come---by chance but once a week,
The pit can witness that you never speak:
Pensive Attention sits with decent mien;
No paint, no naked shoulders to be seen!

And yet this grave, this moral, pious age,
May learn one useful lesson from the stage.
Shun strife, ye fair, and once a contest o'er,
Wake to a blaze the dying flame no more:
From fierce debate, fly all the tender loves,
And Venus cries " Coachman put-to my doves."
The genial bed no blooming Grace prepares,
" And every day becomes a day of cares."

F I N I S.